E
S

Spohn, Kate

Clementine's winter
wardrobe

$13.95

| DATE | |
|---|---|
| APR 3 1991 | DEC 2 4 1992 |
| AUG 1 9 1991 | |
| SEP 0 3 1991 | JAN 1 1 1993 |
| NOV 2 6 1991 | JAN 1 6 1993 |
| | MAY 1 5 1993 |
| DEC 1 0 1991 | OCT 1 2 1993 |
| AUG 1 3 1992 | |
| AUG 2 6 1992 | NOV 2 4 1993 |
| SEP 3 0 1992 | DEC 2 0 1993 |
| JAN 2 9 1994 | JAN 1 1 1994 |
| | MAR 2 1 1994 |
| | JUN 0 7 1994 |

# Clementine's Winter Wardrobe

## BY KATE SPOHN

### ORCHARD BOOKS

A DIVISION OF FRANKLIN WATTS, INC.

NEW YORK

Orchard Books
A Division of Franklin Watts, Inc.
387 Park Avenue South, New York, NY 10016

Orchard Books Canada
20 Torbay Road, Markham, Ontario 23P 1G6
The text of this book is set in 16 pt. Baskerville.
The illustrations are color pencil.
Manufactured in the United States of America
Book design by Sylvia Frezzolini

10  9  8  7  6  5  4  3  2  1

Library of Congress Cataloging-in-Publication Data
Spohn, Kate.   Clementine's winter wardrobe / Kate Spohn.
p.   cm.   "A Richard Jackson book."   Summary: Clementine the cat choses the clothes
she will wear next winter.
ISBN 0-531-05841-7. — ISBN 0-531-08441-8 (lib. bdg.)
[1. Clothing and dress—Fiction. 2. Winter—Fiction. 3. Cats—Fiction.] I. Title.
PZ7.S7636C1  1989        89-42531
[E]—dc19        CIP   AC

FOR BROOKE

Clementine knew winter was coming soon.
*This* year she wanted to be ready.

New clothes were what she needed.

So Clementine thought of longjohns.

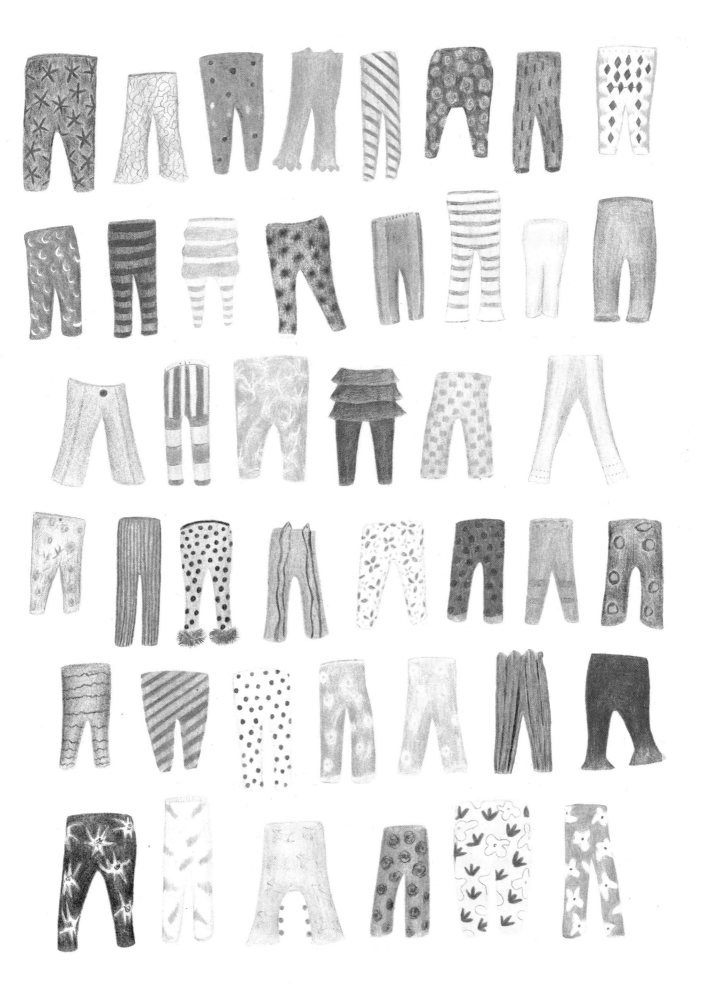

And she thought of shirts,

and jumpers,

and sweaters,

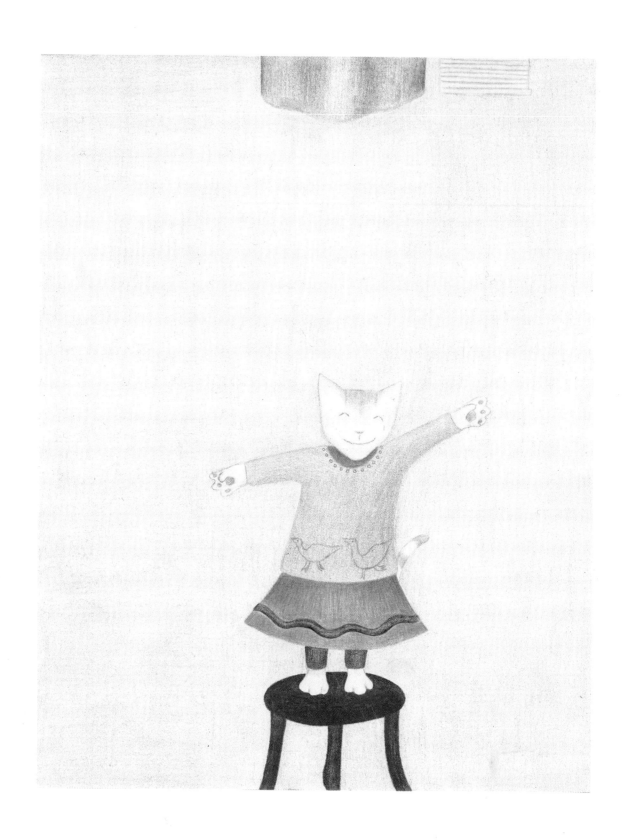

and socks.

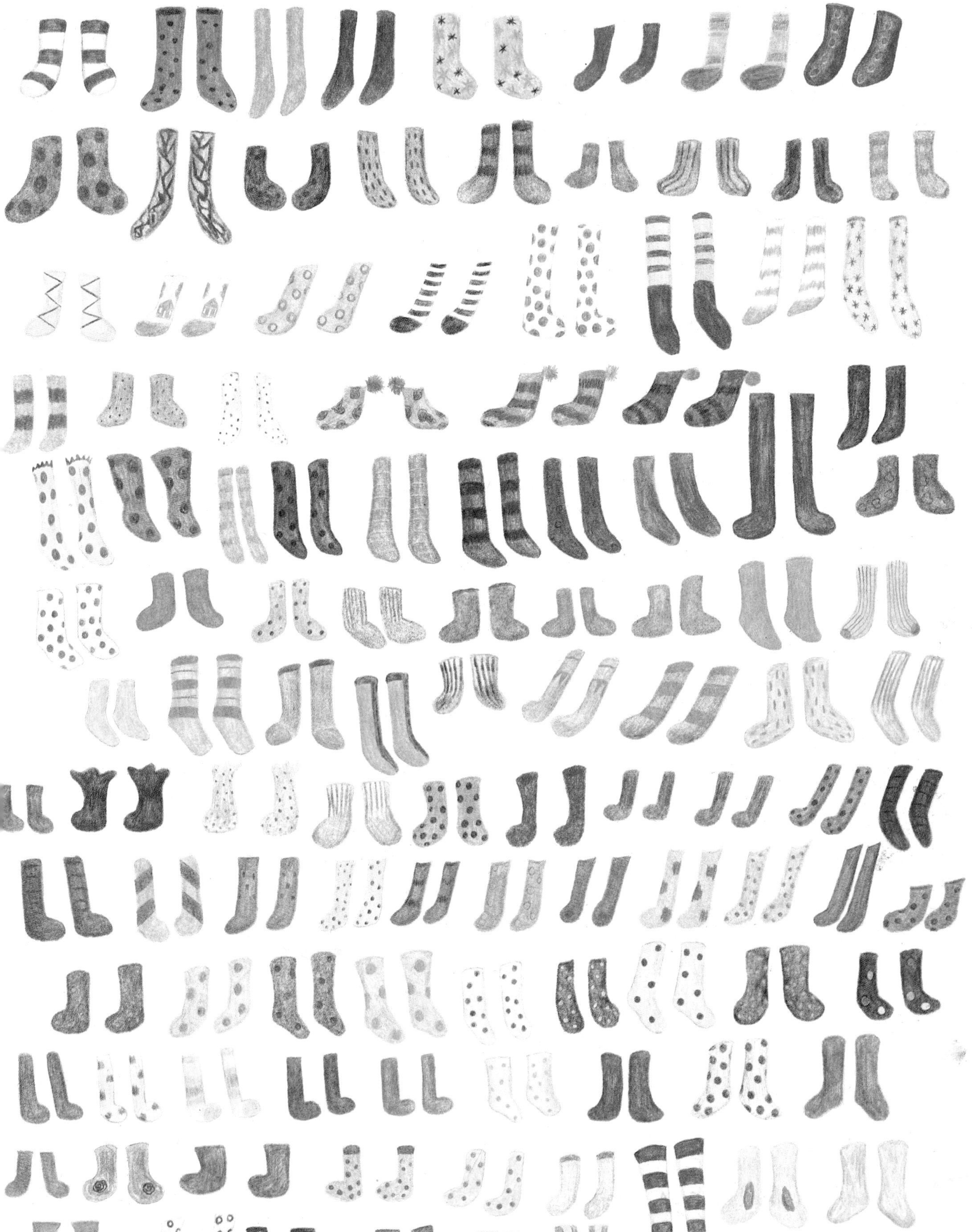

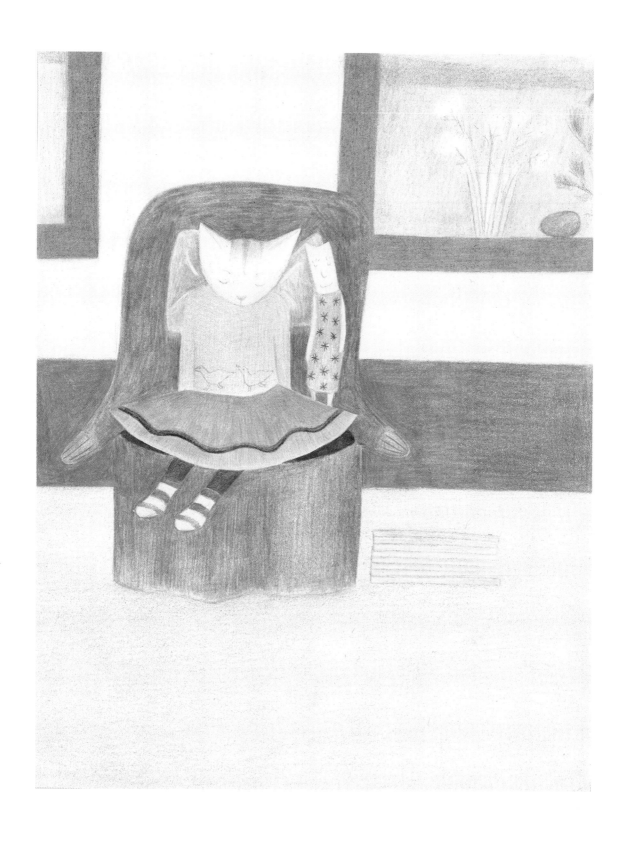

Clementine thought of necklaces,

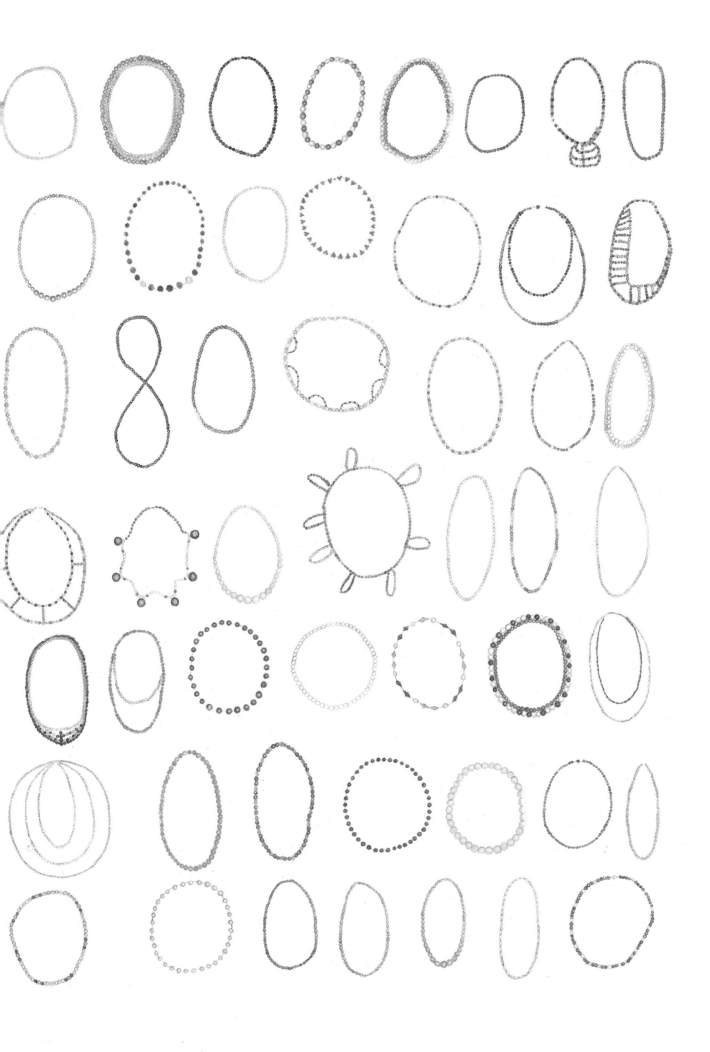

and boots,

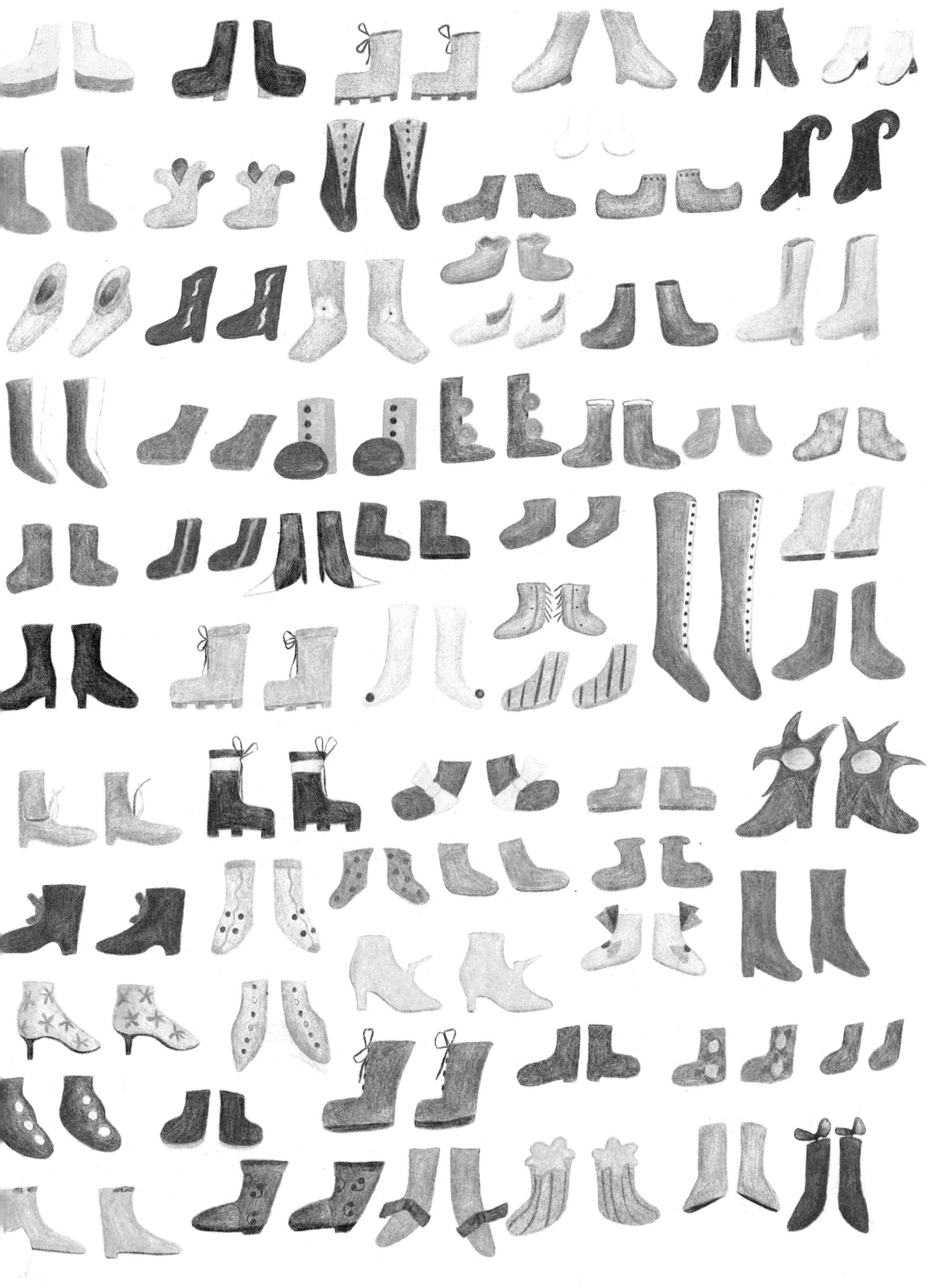

and coats,

and scarves.

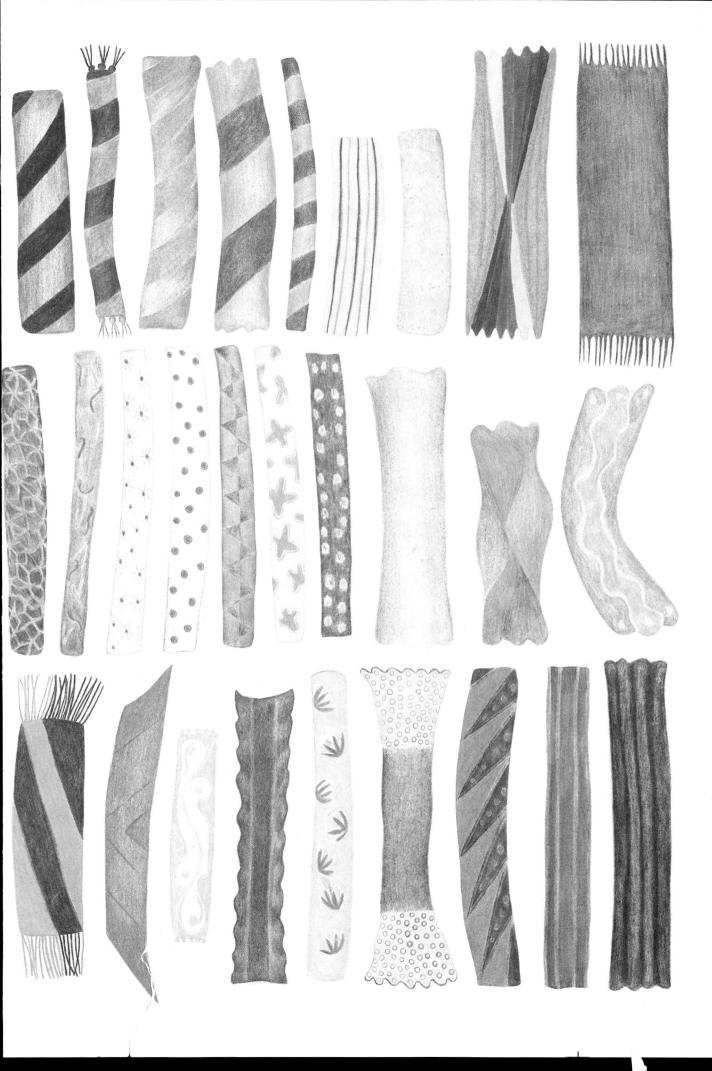

Clementine thought about hats,

and then mittens.

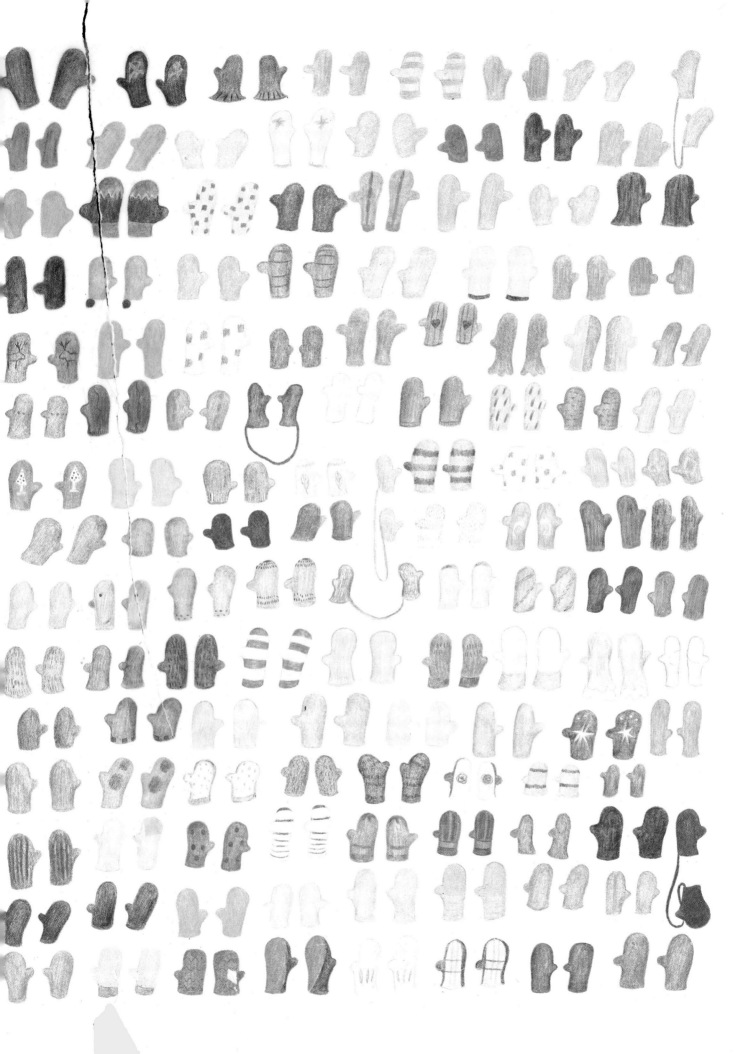

Now Clementine had longjohns, a shirt, a jumper, a sweater, socks, a necklace, boots, a coat, a scarf, a hat, and mittens.

And now Clementine was ready for winter.